W9-BXU-923

TADEO'S SEARCH FOR CIRCLES

By Marion Brooker

Illustrated by Kyrsten Brooker

Fitzhenry & Whiteside

Tadeo searched for perfect circles.
He blew bubblegum beauties
but they popped with a bang.
He built sandcastles with moats in the sand
but waves washed them out to sea.

He yawned goodnight yawns—
but they were not perfect.

That evening, as Tadeo leaned against his fence

dreaming of cowboys,

he threw his rope

into an almost circle

BUT...

...before the end met the beginning
the rope took off with Tadeo,
over the gate, above Senora Madera's mango tree,
past chimneys blowing smoke.

It circled the setting sun—round and hot but not perfect...

...and cruised the blackening sky with its crescent moon
not old, but nearly new—
where Tadeo looped his rope around the tip,
cradled down, and dozed.

In the early, early morning
before the sun was up,
Tadeo stretched, unknotted his rope,
slipped off the moon,
and sped
in and out of clouds until—
a circle!
Tadeo lassoed it…slid down…

But the circle was not quite right...

Tadeo shot right back up
and whizzed…
watching…
and wishing…

...until he saw golden spheres glistening in the sun.

He swooshed down the slope right into…

...a Grand Bazaar!
Tadeo tasted Turkish Delight,
danced to a tanbur,
and sneezed over spices
which sent him whirling and swirling
back up on his rope and away.

Tadeo travelled on and on,
fanning himself against the heat,

hugging himself against the cold

until...

...Tadeo spotted the perfect circle...

perhaps...

He circled lower to see

BUT

...round and round,
faster and faster,
over and over
until...
Tadeo spun off once again
on his search.

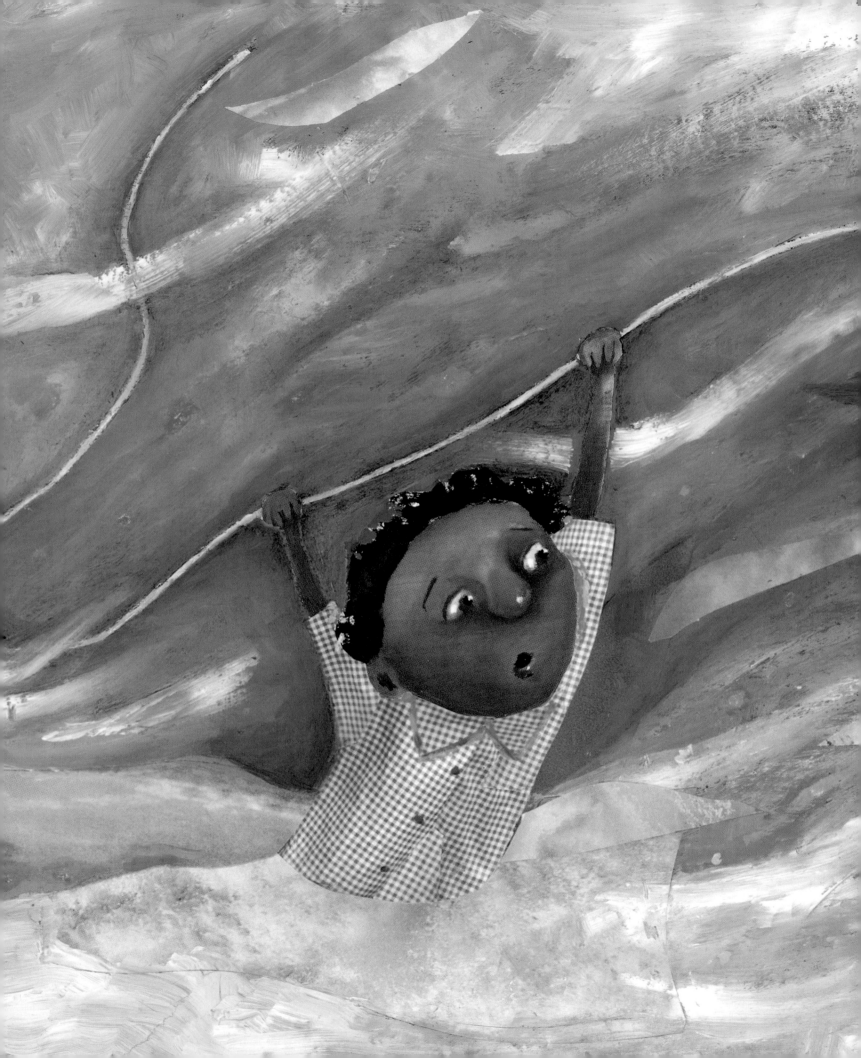

Finally,
way off in the distance, he spotted
something round!

Tadeo
tumbled

down,

down,

but didn't stop!

He fled
across tundra,
skimmed over mountains and
lakes where he saw his shadow,
and twirled across plains and forests.
Then…

...tired,
Tadeo nodded his head on his chest
and spotted
way down below
the PERFECT circle,
the best of all.
He somersaulted down his rope
and lit *kerplunk* inside...

...his mama's arms!

Tadeo yawned and smiled a sleepy smile.
"I've searched from here to there,
and up and down
and all around
and found—

A hug is the most wonderful, perfect circle of all!"

"But a circle's not a hug," his mama whispered,
"until there's someone special in it!"

Published in Canada by Fitzhenry & Whiteside, 195 Allstate Parkway, Markham, Ontario L3R 4T8

Published in the United States by Fitzhenry & Whiteside, 311 Washington Street, Brighton, Massachusetts 02135

www.fitzhenry.ca   godwit@fitzhenry.ca

10 9 8 7 6 5 4 3 2 1

Library and Archives Canada Cataloguing in Publication Brooker, Marion 1932-
Tadeo's search for circles / Marion Brooker, Kyrsten Brooker.
ISBN 978-1-55455-173-6
I. Brooker, Kyrsten II. Title.
PS8553.R65455T34 2011   jC813'.6   C2011-904347-5

Publisher Cataloging-in-Publication Data (U.S)
Brooker, Marion.
Tadeo's Search for Circles / Marion Brooker ; Kyrsten Brooker.
[32] p. : col. ill. ;   24 x 28 cm.
Summary: A young boy's search for the perfect circle takes him on a fantastical journey around the world—only to discover perfection in his own home.
ISBN: 978-1-55455-165-1
1. Shapes – Juvenile literature.   I. Brooker, Kyrsten. II. Title.
[E] dc22   PZ7.B7665Ta   2011

Fitzhenry & Whiteside acknowledges with thanks the Canada Council for the Arts, and the Ontario Arts Council for their support of our publishing program. We acknowledge the financial support of the Government of Canada through the Canada Book Fund for our publishing activities.

Cover and interior design by Daniel Choi
Cover image by Kyrsten Brooker
Printed in Hong Kong, China by Sheck Wah Tong, August 2011, job# 55351

To my children Catherine, Kyrsten, Ian, Delphine – with hugs! M.B.
For Mom & Dad K.B.

Tadeo's Search for Circles

LEGEND

1 - CENTRAL AMERICA
2 - AFRICAN SAVANNAH
3 - ISTANBUL, TURKEY
4 - LONDON, ENGLAND
5 - CANADIAN ARCTIC

WHERE IS "HOME" FOR YOU?

Rocky Mountains

5

1

N
W   E
S